Contents

Frankenstein

Mary Shelley

Retold by Rosie Dickins
Illustrated by
Victor Tavares

Reading Consultant: Alison Kelly
Roehampton University

Designed by Louise Flutter
Series designer: Russell Punter
Series editor: Lesley Sims

First published in 2008 by Usborne Publishing Ltd.,
Usborne House, 83-85 Saffron Hill, London
EC1N 8RT, England.
www.usborne.com

Printed in China. UE.
First published in America in 2009.

Chapter 1

Icebound

In the treacherous waters close to the North Pole, explorer Captain Walton peered over the side of his ship. Only a thin channel of water separated it from the ice.

"Drop the anchor," he ordered his crew. "It's too dangerous to continue... I hope conditions improve soon," he added, under his breath. He knew that if the ice kept thickening, it would crush the ship into matchsticks. Would he ever reach the Pole?

The captain gazed into the distance, wondering what mysteries lay ahead. Suddenly, he blinked. A dog sled had appeared on the horizon.

"Where did that come from?" wondered Walton, staring. "And who is that driving it? He hardly even looks human!"

The sled raced north over the ice and was lost to view.

That night, the sailors were kept awake by eerie noises as ice creaked and rubbed against the ship. By dawn, they saw they were completely surrounded by icebergs – and one carried another dog sled. This time, the driver was definitely a human. But he was a pitiful sight, thin and nearly frozen, and most of his dogs were dead.

Walton and his crew helped the stranger on board and into a cabin, where they brought him warm blankets and hot soup. He was barely alive, but the next night, when he had recovered a little, he began to tell the captain his story.

"My name," he said, "is Victor Frankenstein, and I have suffered greatly. It all began long ago, during my studies..."

As darkness fell and the ice closed in, Captain Walton was held spellbound by Frankenstein's terrible tale...

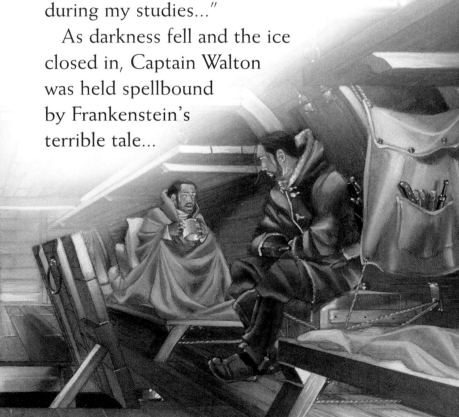

Chapter 2

To create life

From his window, Victor Frankenstein had a fine view over the tiled roofs of Ingolstadt University. But he was too absorbed in his books to notice.

Victor was studying science, hoping to uncover the secrets of the human body. He had always dreamed of making great discoveries. "The world is full of mysteries," he would say. "Who knows what powers we could master, if we only knew how?"

For two years, Victor devoted himself to his work. He went to every class, read every book, and spent hours in the university laboratories. He learned everything his tutors could teach, from how the blood circulates to the nature of the air we breathe.

But there was one question they could not answer, and it tormented Victor. "What is the secret of life itself?" he demanded. And he began to take extra classes in anatomy, and to visit the dead and dying, to try to understand what separates life from death.

One day, Victor came across an article by Galvani, an Italian scientist who had managed to animate a lifeless frog and make it jump, using the power of electricity.

"Could I do the same?" he mused. "Galvani only triggered a brief spark of life and movement; but if I had enough power — say a lightning strike — could I actually create life? Could I make a living being?" And he began to plan a new experiment.

Victor spent months making calculations, building equipment, mixing chemicals, doing tests... He set up a workshop in one of his rooms and barely left it, working feverishly, late into the night.

He was so busy, he hardly wrote home or noticed the changing seasons. Letters piled up, unread, from his family and friends back home in Geneva — his father, his little brother, his best friend Henry and his sweetheart Elizabeth...

From time to time, Victor caught a glimpse of himself in the mirror. Wild-eyed and pale, he was an alarming sight, but he shrugged it off. "I'll take a break as soon as this is over," he promised himself. "I can't stop now."

Completely obsessed, Victor allowed nothing to stand in his way — not even respect for the dead. For his experiment, he needed to build a body. So, by night, he secretly visited dark dissecting rooms and damp graveyards, stealing bones and fragments of flesh. Out of these horrors, he meant to create a completely new creature.

At last, one stormy November night, everything was ready. A flickering lamp sent menacing shadows dancing over the finished body lying on the table. It was a hideous sight, with sunken eyes and shrunken lips. Patches of wrinkled greenish skin barely covered its flabby flesh.

A flash of lightning seared the sky directly overhead, hitting wires Victor had set up on the roof. A vast jolt of energy poured into his equipment, and sent a spark of life into the misshapen creature before him.

Its oversized limbs twitched. Then, it took a hoarse, rattling breath, and its dull yellowy eyes flickered open...

At that moment, Victor saw what he had done. He had meant to create a magnificent new being. But he was face-to-face with a living corpse. He stared in horror.

"I've made a monster," he whispered.

The creature croaked, as if trying to speak, but Victor couldn't understand it. Then it reached out a flabby hand...

Unable to bear it, Victor fled.

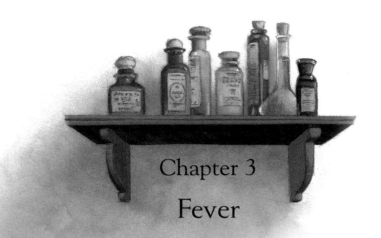

Chapter 3

Fever

Victor spent the rest of the night pacing up and down in the darkness, drenched by rain and tortured by nightmares. He imagined he saw his sweetheart, Elizabeth, but when he embraced her, her skin was cold and maggots crawled out of her clothes...

By dawn, he was sweating and wretched.

"Victor!" called a familiar voice. He turned – and saw his old friend Henry.

"How are you?" asked Henry. "Your family and I have been so worried since you stopped writing that I thought I'd better come and see if you were all right."

Henry paused, noticing how pale Victor looked. "You're not well. I'd better get you home to bed."

Reluctantly, Victor allowed Henry to help him back to his rooms. Steeling himself, he threw open the workshop door with trembling hands. It was empty! There was nothing left of his experiment but a mess of scattered papers and smashed equipment.

"It's gone!" Victor giggled hysterically.

"What's gone?" asked Henry. "Have you been robbed?"

Victor didn't answer. From then on, every noise and shadow filled him with fear. In his exhausted state, the strain was too much. Henry watched in horror as his friend collapsed in a fit.

Victor sank into a fever which lasted for several months. Henry hardly left his side. And slowly, under Henry's care, Victor began to get better.

"A change would do you good," Henry said, when Victor was up and about again. "Let's go away somewhere."

Away from the university, Victor at last relaxed. Henry was careful not to ask about his work, and Victor never mentioned it.

In fact, Victor had decided the monster was probably dead. "It couldn't survive on its own," he told himself. And he did his best to forget all about it.

Chapter 4

Death in Geneva

When Victor returned, there was a letter from his father waiting for him. He opened it eagerly – but his face turned pale as he read...

Dear Victor,

How can I send such bad news? It is with tears and wretchedness I write ~ your little brother William is dead! Murdered! I must tell you how...

We had gone for a family walk in the woods. We stopped to rest and we grown-ups fell asleep. William must have wandered off. When we woke, he was gone.

We searched everywhere. Eventually I discovered his lifeless body, the marks of the murderer's fingers still red around his neck.

A locket containing a picture of his dead mother had been stolen from him. Who could have robbed and killed an innocent child? Surely only a monster, someone without any human feeling!

Hurry home, to comfort us in our grief...

Your loving father

Silently, Victor passed the letter to Henry. "Poor William!" cried Henry. "Still, at least he is at peace now. He does not need our pity – we must keep that for the living."

The friends returned to Geneva by coach. It was a long journey and they arrived late, during a storm. As lightning burned across the sky, Victor spotted a familiar ugly figure in the distance.

"The monster!" He watched it run swiftly over the hills until it disappeared.

Knowing the creature was still alive filled him with despair. "What is it doing here?" he wondered. And the suspicion came to him – could it be the murderer?

The more he thought about it, the more certain he felt. "And I created this thing!" he moaned. "It's my fault it's here. I raised it from the grave, and now it's destroying my own family."

At home, they were greeted by more bad news. The missing locket had been found – in the pocket of William's nanny, a young girl named Justine. For the authorities, eager for someone to blame, that was enough. She had been accused of murder and, after a hasty trial, hanged.

"She couldn't explain how she came to have the locket," sighed Victor's father.

"But I know she was innocent," wept Elizabeth. "She could never have hurt William. She loved him as much as the rest of us."

Victor just shook his head. "I'm sure the monster is to blame for all this," he thought. "But how can I tell them? They'll think I'm insane."

Tortured by remorse, Victor spent hours brooding. No one could comfort him, not even Elizabeth. He felt a terrible guilt for having created such a monster, and lived in fear it would strike again.

To try to distract himself, he went for a long walk in the mountains. He climbed higher and higher, through jagged pines and ragged ravines, until he reached a lonely, rocky slope. Ice glittered in the sunlight and the majestic peak of Mont Blanc towered overhead.

As he gazed up at the mountain, he heard a noise and spun around. A huge, ugly figure had appeared among the rocks. The monster!

"Murderer," cried Victor, trembling with rage. "You strangled my brother, and an innocent woman was hanged for your crime. How dare you come here?"

He sprang to attack – but the monster dodged with inhuman speed and strength, and Victor saw he was powerless against it.

"I thought you would want to kill me," it said fiercely. "But I am stronger than you. Hear me out! Do what I ask, and I will leave you in peace. Listen to my tale before you judge me."

Reluctantly, Victor sat down and the monster began...

Chapter 5

The monster's tale

The first thing I can remember was a bright light. I think it must have been the sun. I followed it until it became too hot, and then I looked around for somewhere to rest.

Eventually I found myself in a forest. I didn't know how to live, and I was miserable. But slowly I learned to eat berries when I was hungry, to drink from a stream when I was thirsty, and to cover myself when it was cold.

I longed for company. One day I met a shepherd, but he ran away. I followed him to his village. It looked like heaven, full of neat cottages and happy people — but the villagers shouted and threw stones to drive me away. I hid in a ruined hut.

From the hut, I could see a remote cottage. An old man and his children lived there. The old man was blind, and his children looked after him.

They were very poor and rarely had enough to eat, but they were always kind to each other.

Sometimes they sang to each other, and I thought it was the sweetest sound there could be. The music filled me with emotions I didn't understand.

Sometimes they read aloud from books. At first I didn't know the words, but slowly I learned.

I longed to be part of their family, but I didn't dare show myself. Instead, I left them gifts of firewood and berries. I admired their faces — they seemed beautiful to me. I was terrified when I saw my own ugliness reflected in a pool of water. No wonder everyone drove me away!

The more I watched the family, the more lonely I felt. I needed company, and I dreamed of meeting them — of winning their friendship with gentle words.

So I decided to approach the old man. Being blind, at least he wouldn't hate the sight of me. I waited until he was alone, then knocked at the door. I told him I was a stranger, and weary, and he invited me to share his fire. He was the first person ever to speak to me with kindness.

But then the children returned and there was no time to explain. They were horrified to see me. The girl fainted, and the boy attacked me. I could have torn him limb from limb, but instead I fled into the woods, howling in misery.

Where could I go? Who would take me in? And then I remembered my creator. My father. You! Surely you would accept me? So I set off to find you.

In a pocket of the coat I was wearing, there were some letters. From these, I knew you came from Geneva, so I made my way there.

In the woods near Geneva, I came across a boy playing. He looked like you. He was so young, I thought he might not yet have learned to hate. I tried to make friends, but he screamed and screamed. I squeezed his throat, to silence him — and killed him.

As he lay at my feet, I noticed a locket around his neck. It was pretty, so I took it.

I knew people would come after the boy, so I looked for a hiding place. Not far away, I found a sleeping woman. She was so young and so lovely, I would have given my life for her — but I didn't dare wake her, in case she screamed too. I had nothing to give her but the locket, so I tucked it into her pocket. Because of this, I heard later, she was executed.

All this happened because I am alone and miserable. No man will be my friend, no woman will love me. I need a companion — a bride. You must make her for me!

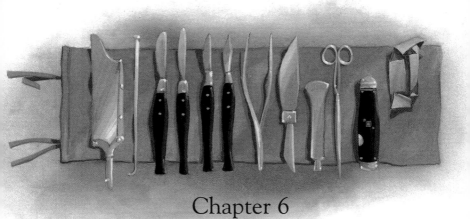

Chapter 6

A monster bride

"Create another creature like you?" cried Victor, appalled. "Never! Together, you might destroy the world."

"You are wrong," replied the monster. "I was good, until misery made me bad. Everyone hates me. Why shouldn't I hate them in return? I am so lonely – but you can help me. Refuse, and I will be revenged. I will make you curse the hour of your birth..." For a moment, rage contorted his features, making him uglier than ever, but he calmed himself and went on.

"Do not deny me this one kindness. Help me be happy, and I will again be good. I will take my bride to live peacefully, far away from people. You will never see us again."

Victor couldn't help feeling sorry for the monster, although the sight of it sickened him. And then there were the threats — the creature was more powerful than any man. It would be safer to do what it asked.

Victor swallowed hard. "I — I agree," he said slowly.

Victor returned home, brooding harder than ever. Elizabeth couldn't bear it.

"Why are you so unhappy?" she asked gently. "Is it because you don't love me any more?"

"No, of course not," cried Victor. "I could never love anyone as much as you. All my hopes for the future rest in you. Elizabeth," he added impulsively, "will you marry me?"

"Oh yes," cried Elizabeth, flinging her arms around him.

But even as Victor kissed her, he was thinking of the monster's demand... "I must start work," he told himself. "But not here! I don't want anyone to know."

Victor's father was delighted when he heard the happy news. "I always hoped you two would marry," he said, smiling. "When shall we hold the wedding?"

"Not for a few months," Victor replied firmly. "I have a project I must finish first."

"I need to make a research trip to — to Scotland," he improvised, trying to think of somewhere quiet and remote.

"A trip will do you good," said Elizabeth. "But I think you should take Henry for company." And so it was agreed.

Victor packed his books and instruments with a heavy heart. A few days later, he and Henry set out. There had been no further sign of the monster, but Victor was sure it would follow them.

The journey took several weeks. Victor was torn between wishing it would take longer, and fearing the monster would think he had given up and begin its revenge.

Along the way, Henry pointed out the sights with delight – rugged hills, ruined castles and spectacular sunsets... But Victor could only think gloomily of the task ahead.

Finally, they arrived in Edinburgh and Victor began collecting supplies. When everything was ready, he told Henry he wanted to travel on alone. "I need to be by myself for a bit," he insisted.

Reluctantly, Henry agreed. "Write to me at once if you need anything," he said.

Free at last, Victor took a boat to a remote, rocky island and rented an old hut.

Then he set to work, mixing chemicals, connecting batteries, beginning his grisly task of shaping flesh and bone...

Victor felt sickened to be doing such work again in cold blood, without the blind confidence he had felt before. Sometimes he could hardly bear to enter the hut. Instead, he paced up and down on the beach, like a restless ghost, while waves dashed against the stones.

He longed to be finished, but he worried if he was doing the right thing. "Will this new creature be as ugly and wicked as the first?" he wondered. "And what will happen if the monsters hate each other? Or if they have children... could they start a new race? Am I buying my own peace by destroying the future of the human race?"

One night, as he worked, Victor happened to glance up at his window. The monster was staring in, watching him. Its lips were wrinkled in an ugly grin, and Victor could have sworn its eyes glowed with spite.

Suddenly, Victor was filled with fury. He began tearing his work to pieces, covering the floor with scraps of bloodied flesh.

The monster howled. "You think you can find a wife and be happy, while I am wretched and alone? But I will have my revenge. I will be with you on your wedding night."

Victor sprang for the door, but the monster was quicker. Moments later, it was disappearing over the water in a boat.

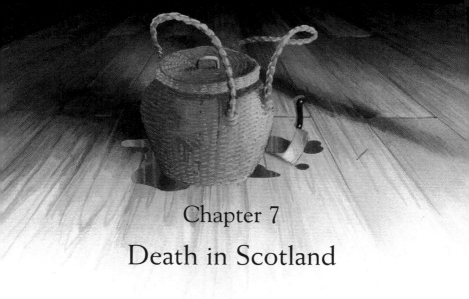

Chapter 7

Death in Scotland

The monster's words rang in Victor's ears: *I will be with you on your wedding night.* "So I'm going to die," he thought. "I'm not afraid." Then he thought of Elizabeth and the grief she would feel. "But I won't go without a struggle."

He stared at the mangled remains of his half-finished creature. It was as if he had murdered a living being. He swept the remains into an old basket, packed up and left the island.

Out at sea, he weighted the basket with stones and flung it overboard.

There was a horrid gurgling as it sank – and then nothing but the stillness of the pure, cold night air. Despite the monster's threats, Victor felt a huge sense of relief. "I'm sure I've done the right thing," he thought.

When Victor landed on the mainland, a crowd gathered around his boat, frowning and muttering. Then a policeman appeared.

"Come with me, sir," he said sternly, gripping Victor's arm. "You have some questions to answer."

"What have I done?" pleaded Victor.

"A man has been strangled," came the reply. "And the murderer was seen making a getaway in a boat like yours."

The crowd parted to let them pass,
revealing something lying on the shore
beyond. It was a body, and its face was
horribly familiar...

"Henry!" Victor gasped. "So it has
begun," he thought despairingly. "The
monster is taking his revenge, and I must
live, while those I love die."

"I didn't kill anyone," he wailed. "It was the monster... the monster I made."

"Really, sir?" replied the policeman, tightening his grip. "Perhaps you'd like to tell the doctor about that."

"He thinks I'm a lunatic," realized Victor. And the rest of what he had been going to say died on his lips.

Victor spent that night in a jail cell, feverishly imagining the monster's next move. "What if it goes back to Geneva?" he muttered. "I've got to protect my family."

Luckily for Victor, a local fisherman had seen him on the island at the time of the murder, proving him innocent. He was released the next morning, and set off for Geneva at once.

His father and Elizabeth greeted him with tears in their eyes. "Thank goodness you're all right," he sighed.

It was a miserable homecoming without Henry. His death, added to William's and Justine's, left a gap that could not be filled.

"But we must get on with our lives," insisted Elizabeth bravely. "Let's set a date for the wedding."

Victor thought again of the monster's threat: *I will be with you on your wedding night.* "Can I really get married now?" he agonized.

"But if I delay, won't the monster just find another means of revenge? And marriage would make Elizabeth happy..."

So, in the end, he agreed.

Chapter 8

Wedding night

Victor did not warn his family about the monster. He was sure they, like the policeman, would think he was crazy. But, as the wedding approached, he became more and more nervous. He carried pistols and a dagger around with him all the time, and was constantly on the lookout.

Elizabeth could see there was something wrong. "What's the matter?" she begged.

"I'll explain after we're married," promised Victor. "I don't want to have any secrets from my wife! But for now, please don't ask questions..."

The wedding took place one sunny morning. It was a small, family affair.

After the ceremony, the newlyweds
set off for a honeymoon in Italy. It was
a beautiful journey, past clear lakes and
calm mountains. It all seemed so
peaceful, Victor began to hope
everything would be all right.
The sun was sinking by
the time they arrived at
their hotel.

Determined to keep Elizabeth safe,
Victor asked her to go upstairs while he
looked around.

He checked everywhere, nervously
fingering his pistol, but there was no sign
of the monster. "Perhaps it's given up," he
thought with relief.

A shrill scream pierced the air. Elizabeth!

He raced upstairs – but he was too late. His beloved wife's pale, lifeless body lay sprawled across their bed, the red marks of her murderer's fingers around her neck.

"Noooo!" he howled.

There was a loud, mocking laugh outside. Victor ran to the window, to see the monster leering up at him from below.

He aimed his pistol at it and fired, but the creature dodged and ran away.

Victor collapsed in sobs, as the hotel staff came running...

When Victor's father heard the news, he was overwhelmed with horror and collapsed. He died a few days later.

Now everyone he loved was dead, Victor longed to die too. He began ranting about monsters, and was locked up in an asylum.

Eventually, he was released. "Now I will have my revenge," he swore, determined to destroy what he had made. "The monster must not be allowed to hurt anyone else. I will pursue it to the ends of the earth..."

Chapter 9

The ice breaks

"I will pursue it to the ends of the earth," repeated Victor to the entranced captain, "and so here I am." His voice faded away, and his head sagged on the pillow. He was at the end of his strength.

Captain Walton got up and went out, closing the door of the cabin behind him. The ship was still imprisoned by ice, and the freezing air struck a chill through his body, though weak sunlight was starting to warm the air a little.

Walton had spent the last few days listening to Victor's story and watching him drift closer to death. "Can it be true?" he wondered. "That strange figure in the distance... was that his monster?"

One thing was certain — Victor wasn't going to make it. He was just too weak. The captain felt sorry for him. From what Victor had said, he had acted stupidly, but not out of wickedness. He had just wanted to make great discoveries.

"Is that so different from me and my ambition to discover the Pole?" Walton wondered. "And will we ever get there?"

As he stood lost in thought, the mountains of ice around the ship began to shift. Then, with a thunderous roar, splits and cracks appeared. The ship would soon be free. The sailors shouted for joy. But over the noise, Walton could hear something else. A voice was coming from the cabin — and it wasn't Victor's.

Walton burst in to find the window open and an ugly creature bent over the bed. It had a hideous face and its skin was greenish and wrinkled, like a corpse. The captain drew a sharp breath. The story was true.

"I came to ask his forgiveness," wailed the monster, its face twisted with grief. "But he was already dead."

Walton looked at the lifeless body on the bed. "Perhaps it's better this way," he thought. "He had so many painful memories."

A sob from the monster made Walton look up again. "But you wanted to kill him," he exclaimed. "Villain! You're not crying because he's dead, but because he's beyond your reach."

"That may be how it looks, but it's not true," replied the monster. "I don't expect you to understand! Hate has ruined me and my dreams. My last victim lies before me. My crimes destroyed him, but they didn't satisfy me. I wanted to be good. I longed for love and friendship, but I knew only hatred and abuse."

"I know I am an outcast and a murderer. You may hate me, but I hate myself more. Only death can end my misery, and I look forward to it."

"What will you do?" asked the captain.

"I will go north," came the creature's reply. "There, I will build a fire and throw myself on the flames — and when it is over, I will finally rest in peace."

Before Walton could move, the monster leaped out of the window. He watched it run swiftly across the ice. Moments later, it was lost in darkness and distance.

Mary Shelley
(1797-1851)

Mary Wollstonecraft Shelley was born in
England in 1797. Her parents were both writers,
and she spent most of her childhood reading,
writing and dreaming.

As she grew up, Mary became friends with
the poets Percy Shelley, whom she later married,
and Lord Byron.

In 1816, the friends spent the summer near
Geneva. Together, they discussed ideas about
good and evil and science, including Galvani's
discovery that electricity could make a dead
body move again — ideas which later made their
way into Mary's writing.

One rainy day, after reading a book of ghost
stories, Byron suggested they each make up a
new ghost story. After a while, the others gave
up. But Mary — inspired, she said, by a terrible
waking dream — went on to write *Frankenstein*.

The novel was published two years later, and
was an instant hit. It was quickly adapted for the
stage, and later film, and has become one of the
most famous stories in the English language.